LIBRARIAN II-BRANCH MANAGER #334878 $24,034-$27,890 (to start). Operate neighborhood branch to include staff supervision, programming, reference and youth services. Prefer exec communication and outreach skills, ability to relate to people from diverse ethnic and socioeconomic backgrounds and interest in African-American literature. Requires MLS from ALA accredited program plus 2 years prof library exp. Send resume w/ SS# to: Grant County Human Resource, P.O. Box 005, Ft. Miles, FL 11198.

in library science, Expe... ence with automated cataloging systems; working knowledge of AACR2, LC rule interpretations and subject headings. Send letter of application to: Cataloger Search Committee, Blander University, Building 23, Room 6, Vernis, RI 09866.

WANTED
Children's Librarian.
Sunrise Elementary School seeks a *thick-skinned* professional to help reduce inventory damage and loss: OUR LIBRARY IS IN DISTRESS! If you possess a *jealous* love of books and a *burning* love of children, Sunrise Elementary wants YOU!
*****
Our new librarian must be on fire with enthusiasm; no halfbaked applicants need apply.

CALL NOW: 555-S.E.A.R.
(Sunrise Elementary Adores Reading).

Public Service Librarians: Children's; Young Adult; for Main Library, New Con... ...ord Public Library. ...H'LDREN'S: Creative librarian to head Children's ...oom. You will enhance ...nd expand vital services ...this multicultural urban ...rary. Required: ALA/ ...S with 5 yrs+ experi... ...ce, in-depth knowledge ...children's literature, ...ng orientation to public ...rvice. Min salary: ...2,397. YOUNG ADULT: ...velop collections and ...grams for teens. As ...t of adult services team, ...will provide general ref... ...nce. Required: 3 yrs ...erience, strong YA ...kground. Min salary. ...933. Resume and ...r: Beverly

dependent progressive coeducational secondary school with an enrollment of 160 (grades 9-12), located in the hills of southwestern Colorado, seek skilled, enthusiastic, in... vative librarian. Resp... sible for administrating op... eration of 26,000 volum... collection, working with P... assistant and student hel... ers, and developing p... to integrate technology i... library service. Qualifi... tions: MLS/ALA with... years experience, prefo... ably in secondary scho... college, practical know... edge of library technolog. Salary range: $18,000 $25,000. Send letter a... resume to Gregg Slat... Dean of Faculty, Th... Farber School, 154 Me... Street, Maple Ridge, C... 55022.

LIBRARIAN II-BRANCH MANAGER #934878 $24,034-$27,890 (to start). Operate neighborhood branch to include staff supervision, programming, reference and youth services. Prefer exec communication and outreach skills, ability to relate to people from diverse ethnic and socioeconomic backgrounds and interest in Af...

Blander University se... Cataloger. Responsi... ties. Under the head, ... cial collections unit, in ... cataloging department... librarian is responsibl... the original catalogin... monographs and non... materials for the follo... collections: govern... documents, reference... riculum, and maps. ... fications required: ... accredited masters d... in library science; ... ence with automate... loging systems: ... knowledge of AAC... rule interpretation ... subject headings.

SPECIAL THANKS

To my family: *Shaun, Katie, Erin, and Lauren for your wonderful ideas; to Ruthann Hendrickson and Don Greene for your puckish sense of fun and great joy in life; to my nephews, Benjamin and Jordan Bendiburg, for making your tia laugh; and to Mami and Papi, of course.*

To media specialists: *Lorry de la Croix, Jane Sullivan, Sherry des Enfants, Harriet Brown, Martha Hooper, Rita Linker, Julie Strickland, Betty Beasley, Karen Haglund, Carol Harless, Betty Brown, Ellen Limbrick, and the Miss Lottys of the Norcross Public Library.*

– C.D.

*Thanks to my wife, Traci, to my mother,
and to all my family and friends for your belief in my work.*

– M.W.

ISBN 0-590-97905-1

Text copyright © 1994 by Carmen Agra Deedy.
Illustrations copyright © 1994 by Michael P. White.
All rights reserved. Published by Scholastic Inc., 555 Broadway, New York, NY 10012, by arrangement with Peachtree Publishers, Ltd.

12 11 10 9 8 7 6 5 4 3 2 1   6 7 8 9/9 0 1/0

Printed in the U.S.A.   14

First Scholastic printing, October 1996

The Library Dragon

Carmen Agra Deedy

ILLUSTRATED BY
MICHAEL
P. WHITE

SCHOLASTIC INC.

NEW YORK   TORONTO   LONDON   AUCKLAND   SYDNEY

*This book is dedicated to Cherrie Smith, who has known all along
that in the library beats the heart of the school.*

And to Robin DeFoe, who is like a sister.

— C.D.

*To my father, who taught me that the true meaning of a man is not
power or strength, but how he treats all people. I miss you.*

— M.W.

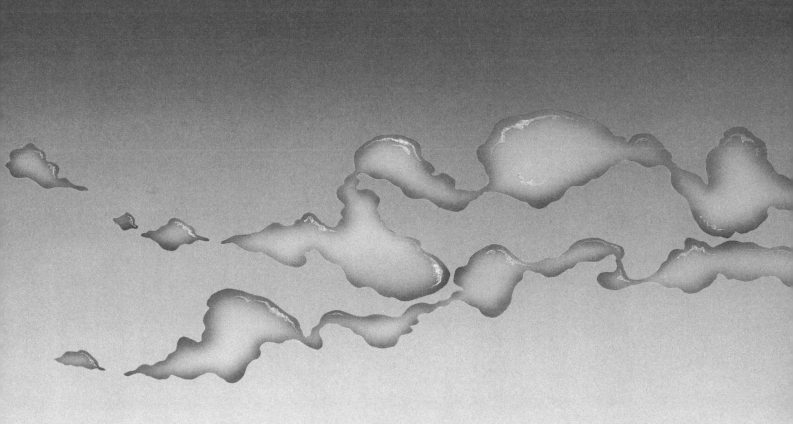

Sunrise Elementary School had a BIG problem.
The new librarian, Miss Lotta Scales, was a *real dragon*.

Miss Lotta Scales was hired to guard the Library. And she took her job seriously: hundreds of new, clean books replaced the old, smudged ones. These shining gems neatly lined the shelves of her library lair in perfect order — no 398.2s in the 500s, and absolutely no fiction among the biographies.

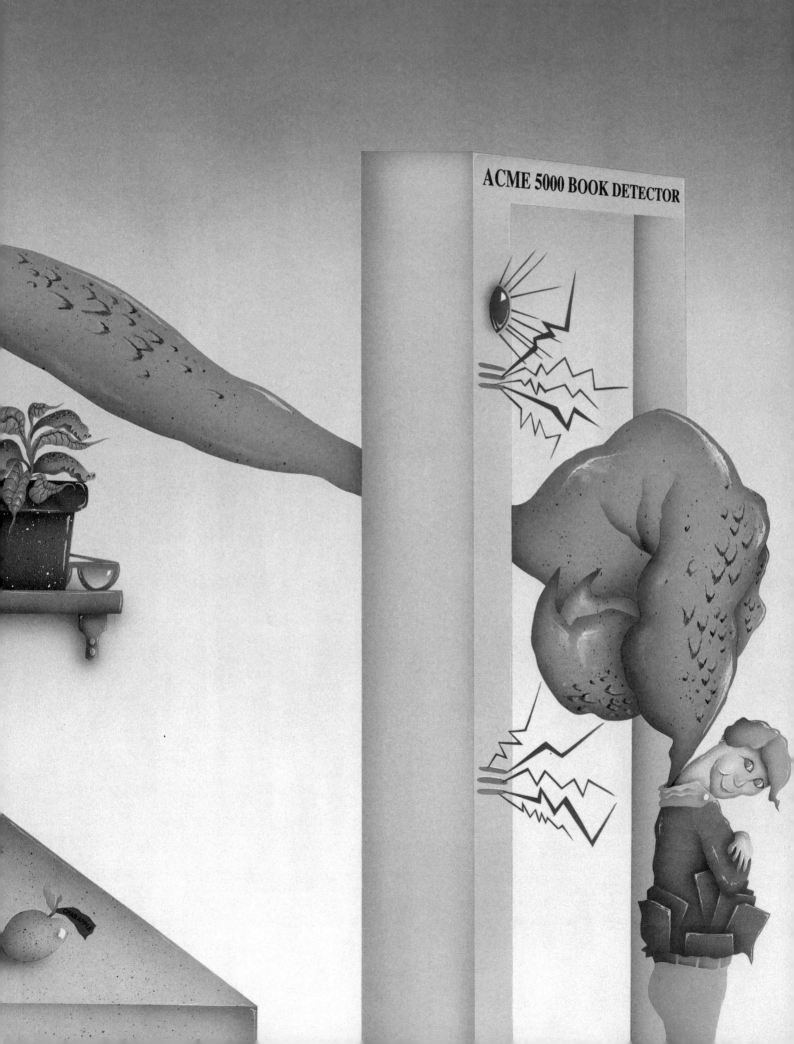

She kept a fiery eye out to make sure no one removed
any books from the shelves. Her motto was,
　　　"A place for everything, and that's where it *stays*."
The very thought of sticky little fingers

touching
and
clutching,

pawing
and
clawing,

smearing
and
tearing

her precious books just made her hot under the collar.

Miss Scales thought that the way some books spread an unfounded fear of dragons was positively inflammatory.

"Books that depict cruelty to dragons should never have been published in the first place."

She got so fired up about this, she didn't just discard the books she didn't like, she *incinerated* them.

The kids watched in awe.

"Well, that settles it," whispered Albert Hoops. "Where there's smoke, there's fire, and that Miss Scales is a *real dragon*, all right."

PTA MEETING

Topic:
"Dragons Throughout History:
The Myth, the Mystery"

Speaker: Sir Whyte Knight

**IF ALARMED,
PULL TAIL**

Not surprisingly, the kids at Sunrise Elementary
School began to dread Library Day.

It wasn't long before the teachers stopped sending
the children to the Library: they kept coming back singed.

First, the principal tried
to reason with Miss Scales,
but his plan backfired.
Instead of cooling her down,
he just fanned the flames.

"And finally, don't forget who does the hiring, Miss
Scales," sputtered the principal.

"Oh really? And who does the *firing*?" asked Miss Scales
with a glare and a flare that caught his tie on fire.

"Now cut that out," said the principal as he waved the
smoke out of his face.

"No smoking in the Library," Miss Lotta Scales said drily.

The principal fumed. The teachers were incensed. Worst of all,
the children had missed reading and storytime for weeks and their
grades were going up in smoke.

So, the teachers formed a delegation. And after a trip to the
cafeteria kitchen to fortify themselves, they paid a visit to Miss Scales.

Miss Lotta Scales smouldered as she listened to sweet Miss Lemon the kindergarten teacher.

"...and most importantly, Miss Scales, dear, the children miss storytime."

"Storytime, shmorie-time," blew Miss Lotta Scales, "why, if I let the children touch these books with their gooey fingers and snotty noses, this Library wouldn't last a week."

And she stared so furiously at the teachers that they threw down their weapons and clanged out. All except sweet Miss Lemon.

"You know, Miss Scales, we all love the books as much as you do..., but *the Library belongs to the children.*"

"Good Knight, Miss Lemon, you slay me," cracked Miss Scales. "Why the idea of storytime is simply *medieval.*"

As usual, the dragon had the last word.

"That Miss Lemon is a real spitfire," chuckled Miss Scales. But she had spewed so much smoke and fire at sweet Miss Lemon that she had to lie down for a nap. She was really draggin'. In fact, she was burned out.

"Being a Library Dragon can be such a lonely job," she mumbled sadly to herself as she heaved a mighty sigh and closed her scaly lids.

It was at that very moment that Molly Brickmeyer
accidentally wandered into the Library.

CRAB APPLE

Snuff The Magic Dragon

Molly was on a quest: she had lost her glasses and
couldn't see a thing without them unless it was right
under her nose. She stumbled into a bookshelf and a
book fell onto her lap. She never saw the sign
that read,

Do Not Touch The Books
For Display Only

It was over her head.
So she held this one right under her nose
and began to read out loud.

First a class of second graders, in line for the water
fountain, heard her and tiptoed in to listen.
Then, the fourth graders, outside playing kickball,
heard a story being read and crowded around
the windows.

"Speak up," someone said.
Molly Brickmeyer spoke up.
Word of storytime in the Library spread like
wildfire at Sunrise Elementary School.

Everyone
was listening.
Even the
Library Dragon.

And her ears
were burning.

Slowly Miss Lotta Scales rose up from behind a bookshelf and looked at the boys and girls huddled around Molly. She'd never seen anything quite like it: *the children looked like they belonged here.*

"'…I love you, Snuff,'" Molly read on as all the children listened.

"Give me that book, Molly Brickmeyer," roared Miss Scales.

Molly held the book cheerfully toward the scaly blur.

Miss Lotta Scales took the book and eyed it suspiciously as it hung from her claw. First she sniffed it. Then she checked the spine for cracks. Then she checked each page for stains and smudges.

Finally Miss Scales looked around at the children and cleared the smoke from her throat.

"Now, where were we? Why, yes, … 'I love you, Snuff…'"

At first the children were too nervous to listen. But when Molly Brickmeyer climbed up onto Miss Lotta Scales's lap—and didn't get scorched—they relaxed.

"You're warm," whispered Molly.
"Don't interrupt," Miss Scales crackled.

Everyone was listening so intently that they almost missed it: as she read, Miss Lotta Scales's scales began to fall on the linoleum floor with a clickety-clack, clickety-clack, . . .

…clickety-clack—until all that was left was Miss Lotty, librarian and storyteller, sitting on a mountain of yellow, green, and purple scales with Molly Brickmeyer, Dragon Slayer Extraordinaire, on her lap.

The rest of the children warmed up to Miss Lotty right away.

The changes in Miss Lotty's new kid-friendly library
were hard to miss. Not surprisingly, the kids at Sunrise
Elementary School began to *love* Library Day.

Miss Lotty's transformation, however,
was not complete . . .

MIND YOUR LIBRARY MANNERS
• Treat a book like you treat a friend– you don't wipe your nose on your friend.
• Remember to check hurt books into our Book Hospital
• Return books when due, so others can enjoy. (This is a library, not a bookstore!)
• If you need help, ask! (That's why I get paid the big bucks.)
• Quiet, please. (Whisper in the library; yell on the playground.)
Happy reading, pumpkins!
ERFLY LILIES
Rubbish Pile
SWEET PEAR
Miss Lotty
(LIBRARY GODDESS)
OPEN BOOKS
OPEN MINDS

But then, every librarian needs to be a little bit of a dragon —
or else,
WHO WOULD GUARD THE BOOKS?

THE END OF
OUR
TALE